BUT I DON'T EAT ANTS

WRITTEN BY

DAN MARVIN

ILLUSTRATED BY

KELLY FRY

POW!

BROOKLYN, NY

IN MEMORY OF THE WOMAN WHO FIRST
FILLED MY HEAD WITH STORIES: SUSAN C. MARVIN
–DAN

BUT I DON'T EAT ANTS

TEXT © 2017 DAN MARVIN
ILLUSTRATIONS © 2017 KELLY FRY

PUBLISHED BY POW!
A DIVISION OF POWERHOUSE PACKAGING & SUPPLY, INC.
32 ADAMS STREET, BROOKLYN, NY 11201-1021

INFO@POWKIDSBOOKS.COM   WWW.POWKIDSBOOKS.COM
WWW.POWERHOUSEBOOKS.COM   WWW.POWERHOUSEPACKAGING.COM

LIBRARY OF CONGRESS CONTROL NUMBER: 2017944451

ISBN: 978-1-57687-837-8

BOOK DESIGN: KRZYSZTOF POLUCHOWICZ

10 9 8 7 6 5 4 3 2 1

PRINTED IN MALAYSIA

I AM AN ANTEATER
AND I LOVE TO EAT.

BREAKFAST. LUNCH. DINNER.

BUT
I DON'T
EAT
ANTS.

APPETIZERS.
SNACKS.
DESSERT.

BUT I DON'T EAT ANTS!

FAST FOOD.

FINGER FOOD.

FANCY FOOD.

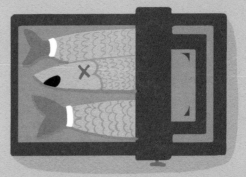

I WILL EAT WITH AN ANT,
BUT I DON'T EAT ANTS.

STRUDELS? NOODLES?
I'LL EAT OODLES.

**I ENJOY ITALIAN ANTIPASTO,
BUT I DON'T EAT ANTS!**

I'LL GOBBLE
GAZPACHO
BY THE GALLON.

GAZPACHO

I'LL DEVOUR DEVILED EGGS BY THE DOZEN.

I'LL EAT
"ANTS ON A LOG,"

BUT I DON'T EAT ANTS.

**KOALAS AREN'T CALLED
EUCALYPTUS-EATERS.**

**PANDAS AREN'T CALLED
BAMBOO-EATERS.**

**JAGUARS EAT ANTEATERS,
BUT THEY AREN'T CALLED ANTEATER-EATERS.**

**MY ANTEATER AUNTS EAT ANTS,
BUT I DON'T EAT ANTS!**

IT'S DINNER TIME.

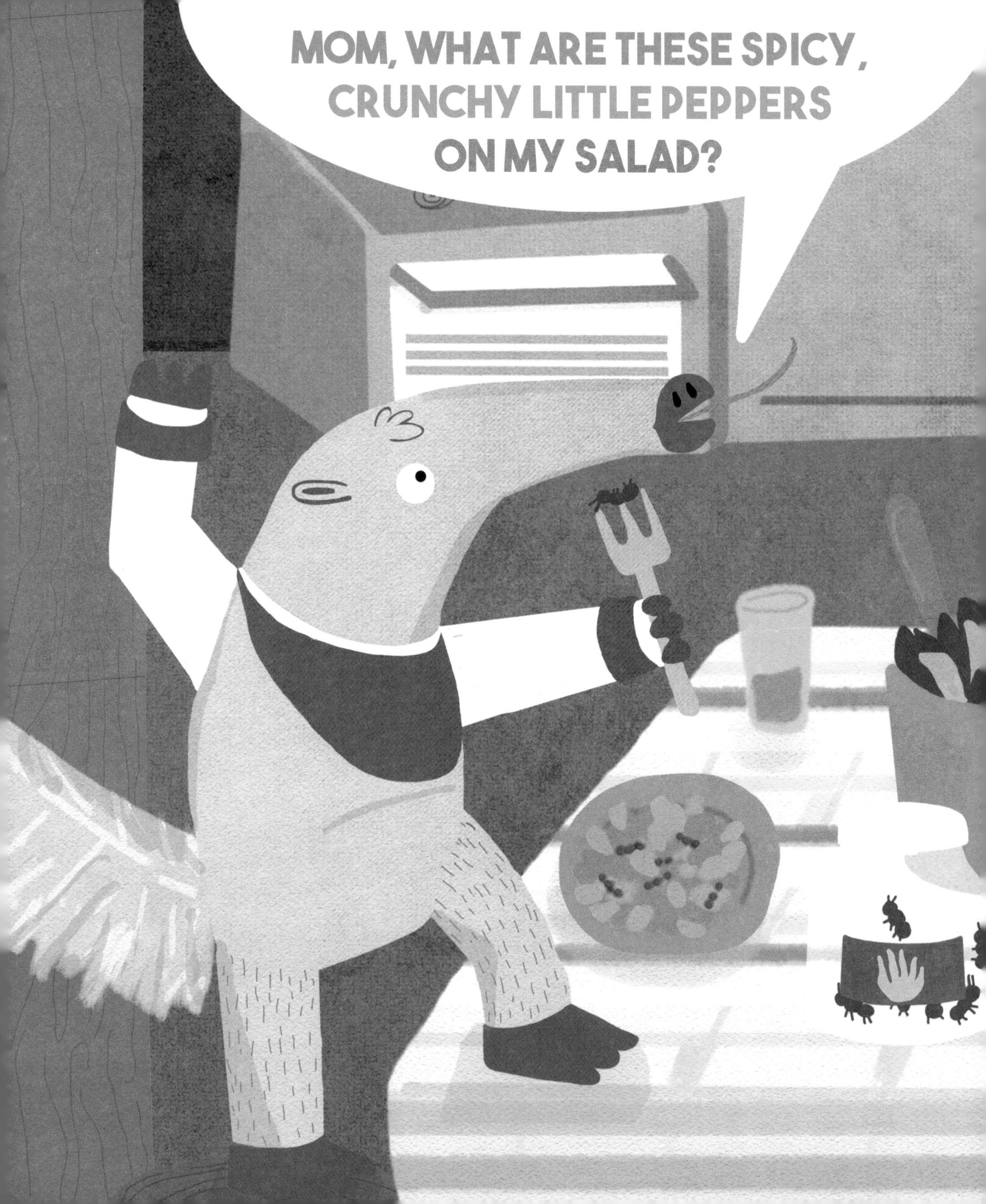
MOM, WHAT ARE THESE SPICY, CRUNCHY LITTLE PEPPERS ON MY SALAD?

THEY'RE MORE APPETIZING THAN ANY APPETIZER. MORE DELECTABLE THAN DEVILED EGGS. TASTIER THAN TORTELLINI. I COULD EAT THEM EVERY DAY, ALL THE TIME. SO, WHAT ARE THEY?

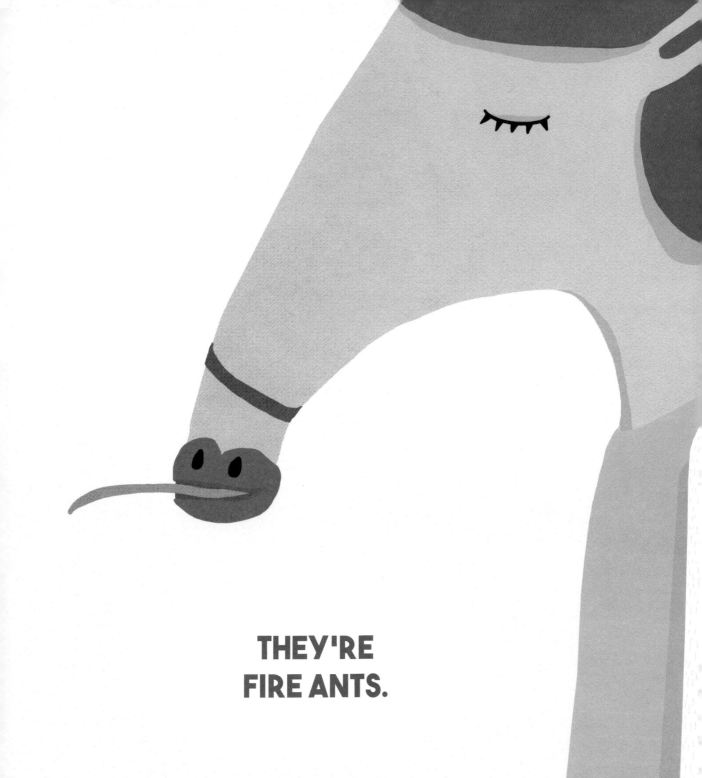

**THEY'RE
FIRE ANTS.**

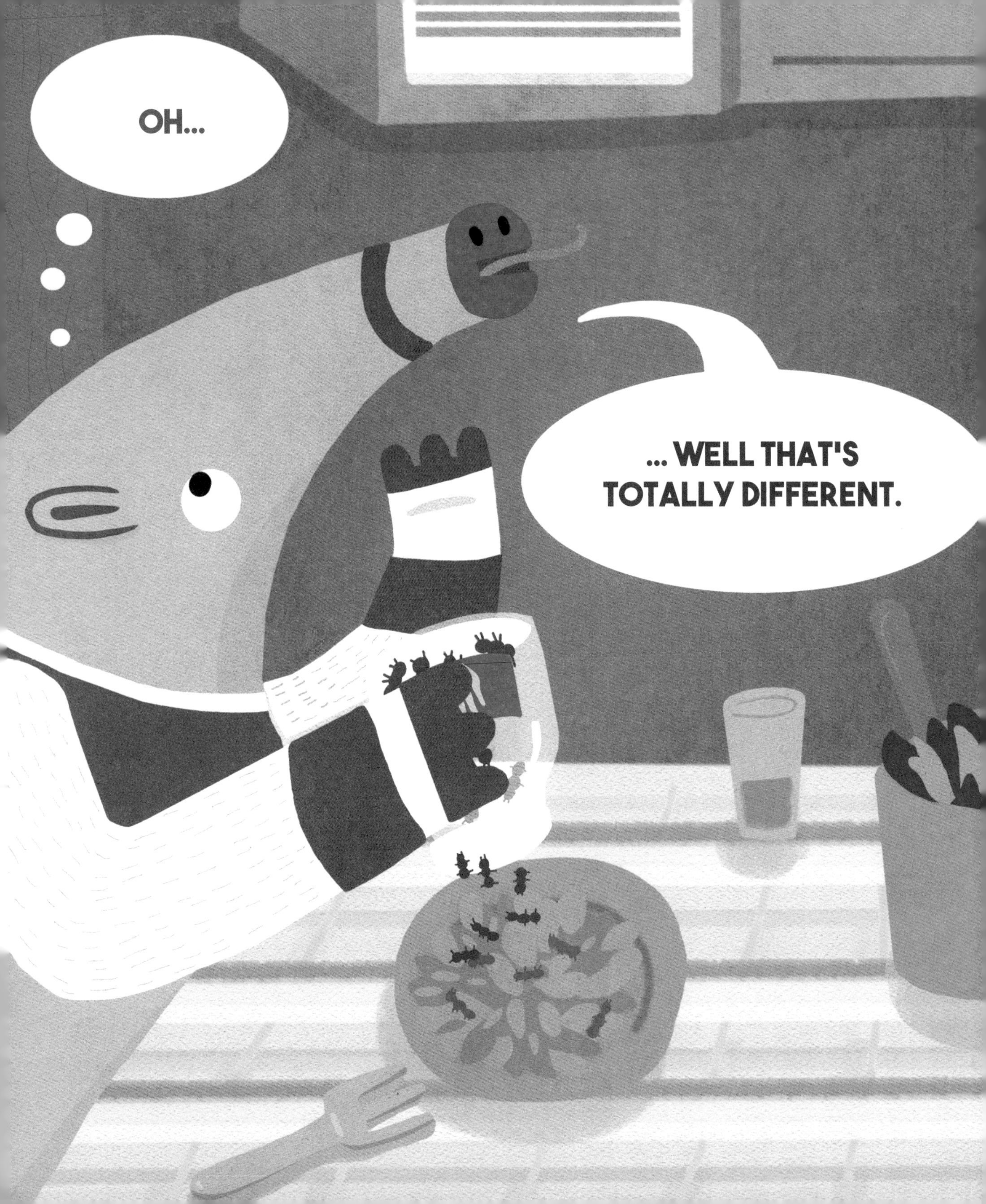
OH...
... WELL THAT'S TOTALLY DIFFERENT.